TOM NICOLL

LEVEL UP!
LAST ONE STANDING

ILLUSTRATED BY
ANJAN SARKAR

LiTTLE TiGER
LONDON

LEVEL 1

My mum had just fallen out of an aeroplane. How's your day going?

   To be honest, things like this had become quite normal for me and my best friend Max, ever since the two of us found ourselves trapped inside a series of video games. So far we had been space soldiers, block people and creature coaches. But it had always been just the two of us trapped in the games.

Until now.

The latest game we had jumped into was *Last to Leave* – the world's most intense Battle Royale survival game – and for reasons currently known only to her, Mum had joined us. I'd have asked her why but as I mentioned, SHE HAD JUST FALLEN OUT OF AN AEROPLANE.

"Flo, what are we going to do?" yelled Max above the roar of the plane's engine and the noise from the other players.

"We need to go after her," I said, grabbing hold of his arm.

"And how do we do that? By jumping out of the plane?" He began to laugh but stopped when he saw my expression. "You can't be serious!" he shouted.

I looked him straight in the eye. "Max," I said. "You've known me all your life. Does jumping out of a plane sound like something I'd try to get you to do?"

Max considered this for a second. "Well, yes, it does actually."

"Exactly," I said. "So stop wasting time. Besides, you've got a parachute on."

"Do I?" he said, looking over his shoulder. "Oh yeah. Where did that come from?"

"I don't know," I said. "Everyone just gets one."

Getting to the front of the plane wasn't proving as easy as I had hoped, given the urgency of the situation. A blockade of players had formed as they all lined up to jump out. I elbowed and pushed my way past them until Max and I were at the door, but when I scanned the island below us I couldn't see any sign of Mum.

I turned to Max, whose eyes were like giant saucers. Normally this would be the point when I'd

try to calm him down, give him some encouragement and tell him everything was going to be OK. But that would take time we didn't have. The longer we left it, the further we'd be from Mum and the harder it would be to find her. So I did the only thing I could do.

I shoved Max out of the plane. And following the sounds of his screams, I dived after him.

I should probably have told him how to open his parachute.

As we plummeted towards the ground, I used the time to remind myself of the *Last to Leave* map. In the north were the snow-covered mountain peaks of the Arctic Zone. The green trees of the Jungle Zone lay to the west and in the south were the sand dunes of the Desert Zone. Green hills and meadows formed the Grasslands to the east and in the centre of the map, where we were headed, were the quaint cottages and picturesque villages of the Olde Zone.

I was worried at seeing all the other players landing in positions around the map. *Last to Leave* was a battle to survive. Only one team could win.

With the ground racing towards us, I pulled the cord on my parachute, slowing my fall. Moments later I was relieved to see Max open his own chute. I'd known he'd figure it out! I was slightly less relieved when he proceeded to fly right into a clock tower. "OW!" I heard him yell.

I landed in the middle of the village square and my parachute vanished, as video game parachutes tend to do. I looked up at Max, who was dangling helplessly about thirty feet above ground, his parachute caught in the tower's spire.

"Max, release your parachute," I shouted.

"How do I do that?" he asked.

Parachutes usually disappeared once players hit the ground. If you got stuck, you could press the X key to cut yourself free but that wasn't an option here.

"Is there a button or something on the chute you could press?" I asked. "Some kind of catch maybe?"

"Not that I can see," he said. "Also if I do get free, I'm not super keen on the massive drop that comes afterwards."

"One problem at a time, please, Max," I said, looking around the square for inspiration. But while the cobblestone streets and quiet shops and cafes looked positively charming, they didn't really offer much in the way of a solution to Max's problem.

So, in a way, it was handy when the lasers started firing.

Pew-pew!

The blast cut right through Max's chute and he dropped like a rock, straight into my open arms. This was a video game though, so unlike a rock he weighed nothing at all.

"Thanks," he said.

Another blast shot past my head, then suddenly four more players were in the square with us. Two boys and two girls, all wielding impossibly large laser cannons. Pointed our way.

"We'd better go," I said.

"I was thinking that," agreed Max.

I started sprinting across the square, shots nipping at my heels as I ran.

"You could put me down," yelled Max.

"No time," I shouted back.

I ran through the open doorway of a run-down post office and kicked the door shut before dumping Max on the ground.

"Come on, we need to find the back exit," I said. "They won't be long."

I was right. I had just lifted up the serving hatch of the post-office counter when the front door burst open. A mean-looking boy with neon-green spiky hair, wearing desert camouflage trousers and a white tank top, stepped inside.

"Hiding in the post office, eh?" He laughed.

"Well, I've got a special delivery for you right here."

He raised his laser cannon and opened fire. Max and I dived behind the counter as the wall behind us exploded, leaving a huge hole.

"Oh wow," I said. "I didn't know they'd added destructible environments to this game. Cool."

"I'm not sure this is the time to be admiring the game's new features," said Max.

"Good point," I said. "Though with any luck it might give us a way out of here. Listen!"

A *click-clack* sound was coming from the other end of the room.

"He's reloading," I said. "Let's go."

Max and I sprang to our feet, then dived through the hole. It brought us out into a narrow alley.

"Which way?" asked Max.

His question was quickly answered when another member of the attacking squad appeared at the end of the alley – a girl this time, wearing dark sunglasses and a full-length purple coat.

"Run, little bunnies, run," she cackled.

We took her advice and ran in the opposite direction, then turned right into a lane and headed along a row of back gardens.

"In here," I said, opening the third gate we reached. As Max pushed past me into the garden, I glanced up the lane but there was no one there. Yet. I closed the gate, then Max and I headed into the house and went straight upstairs, each step squeaking beneath us as if they were trying to give us away. We entered what was clearly a nursery, with a cot, and pictures of balloons and teddy bears on the walls. Carefully, we crept towards the window. There wasn't much to see beyond a few more similar-looking houses and a small garage sandwiched between them. Carmack's Cars.

Max was about to speak when I held up my hand and we moved away from the window. I could hear footsteps outside.

"Where'd they go?" asked the girl we had seen in the alley.

"Dunno," replied the boy from the post office. "But they can't have gotten far."

"They might have found equipment by now," said a new voice, another girl. "Weapons even. We should bounce."

"You're right," said a fourth voice. "And look, we've got wheels."

I chanced a peek out of the window. He was right. There in the garage was an open-top truck. Vehicles were invaluable in this game so it was a shame we hadn't gotten to it first, but I couldn't help feeling relieved as the four of them climbed into the truck, two in the cab at the front and two riding in the back with an assortment of wooden crates.

"It's OK, we're safe," I said as the truck pulled out of the garage and turned on to the lane. Max breathed a long sigh as he looked out of the window.

Then we saw her.

Crouching down, hidden from the other team by the crates, was Mum. Travelling further away by the second.

LEVEL 2

"Hey, come back!" I shouted at the truck as it disappeared down the lane towards the edge of the village.

"I doubt they can hear you," said Max.

"Of course they can't," I said. "But what else are you meant to shout when your mum gets taken hostage?"

"To be fair, I don't think they've noticed her yet," said Max. "I'm not sure you can really be someone's hostage if they don't actually know you exist."

"That's just a technicality," I said. "They're bound

to discover her soon and then she'll be their hostage."

"Won't they just shoot her?" asked Max.

"Well, yes, so she'll only be their hostage for a short while," I admitted. "It doesn't matter, we're wasting time here. We need to go after her."

Max looked out of the window. "Where? They've gone and I don't exactly remember them announcing their destination."

"The map!" I cried.

"What map?" asked Max.

I didn't reply. I was too busy searching my clothes for any sign of a map stuffed up a sleeve or inside a pocket. The island in *Last to Leave* was huge – although I had played the game a lot, I still hadn't seen it all. Navigating it without a map was unthinkable.

Normally you could access the map by pressing

the M key. There had to be an equivalent action Max and I could do now.

After a minute of frantically searching, I still didn't have a map. I glanced at my watch. Time was ticking away and…

"Hang on," I said. "Where did this watch come from?"

Max looked at his own wrist. "Oh yeah, I've got one too," he said.

"I wonder if…" I said, pressing the watch face.

Suddenly a huge holographic map beamed out of the watch, showing the entire island as I remembered it from playing in the real world.

"Woah!" said Max.

In the middle of the map was a clump of brown houses labelled with the words 'Olde Zone'. In one of the houses were two round blue markers.

"That's us," I said, pointing at them. Then, running a finger up the road that led out of the village, I came across a third marker, another blue one, moving at some speed.

"It's Mum!" I said. "It has to be."

"It shows you where she is?" asked Max.

"Normally it only shows you and your team," I said. "Unless … of course. Mum must be paired up with us. I guess since she entered the game on the same account it must have automatically grouped us. This is great – now we know where to find her. It looks like they're heading north to the Arctic Zone. Come on, let's go."

"Right," said Max, looking anxious. "I'm all for finding your mum, but that team had lasers, Flo. And, well, not to put too fine a point on it – we don't! Shouldn't we—"

"You're right! What was I thinking? Of course we should search this place for equipment," I said.

"Actually I was going to say shouldn't we just hide out?" said Max. Perhaps it was my frown that made him add, "But I suppose your plan works as well."

"Besides," I said, opening a wardrobe and finding nothing, "hiding isn't really an option in Battle Royale games. Not for long anyway. At some point soon the map is going to start shrinking, and when it does, we'll need to make sure we don't get left behind. What's important now is that we find some decent loot, to give us a fighting chance against the other players."

"I assume by 'decent', you don't mean this?" said Max, lifting up a soup pot from underneath the cot.

"Oh no, that's good," I said. "You can use pots as helmets. I mean, they're not as good as actual helmets but they're better than nothing. Try it on."

An unimpressed Max reluctantly put the pot on his head.

He looked ridiculous.

"Suits you," I lied, trying to conceal a smirk. "There's nothing else here though. Let's try another room."

"Who leaves pots in a baby's room anyway?" grumbled Max to himself as we walked next door to what seemed to be the master bedroom.

"Now we're talking," I said, picking up a small laser pistol from a dresser. It was barely bigger than my hand but at least it would give us a chance in a firefight. There were also a couple of small blue cylinders next to it – extra laser batteries – that I pocketed too.

"What about this?" asked Max, picking up an empty mug. "Can we use this?"

"Yeah, sure," I said. "You can use that as a melee weapon or a projectile."

Max waved the cup in the air as if trying it out. "Oh, hey, there's a clock here. Should I take that as well? Although I have a watch for telling the time so…"

"No! You should take the clock!" I said, perhaps too eagerly. "They're … um … handy for—"

CREAK!

Max and I looked at each other. Someone was coming up the stairs and there was no time to get out of the room. We were cornered.

CREAK!

"Quick, hide," I said, closing the door. I flipped over the bed to create another barrier between us and whoever was coming.

From behind the bed I aimed my laser pistol at the door.

"Should I use my mug?" Max whispered.

"Don't be daft," I said. "It's just a mug."

"But you said—" he started.

CREAK!

"I was just trying to make you feel a bit safer considering we only have a pistol between us," I said.

"I suppose the pot is useless too," he said.

"No, actually I was telling the truth about that," I said. "It's an odd game."

"And the clock?" asked Max.

CREAK!

"Shh," I said.

I could hear footsteps outside the room now. Then silence, except for the rapid breathing coming from Max. I, on the other hand, was strangely calm but somehow excited too. I loved the tension in Battle Royale games. I just had to avoid thinking about how high the stakes were in this one.

Then the door burst open and I let loose, unloading a full battery of laser charge into the hall.

I ducked back down, taking cover while I reloaded the pistol with a new battery.

"Did you get them?" asked Max.

"Not sure," I said.

"No, she didn't," laughed a voice from outside the room. It was a boy's voice and strangely familiar. "But I think this hall might need some redecorating."

"Flo, doesn't that sound like…" began Max, but I had already stood up as the boy entered the room, pointing a laser pistol of his own right at me. When he saw me, he stopped dead in his tracks. While the expression on his avatar didn't change, I knew for certain that in the real world his mouth was wide open.

LEVEL 3

I fired first.

Hodges – Rhett Hodges, complete with his trademark sneer and black fringe – fired second.

We both missed. Hodges rushed back into the hallway as I dived behind the bed.

"Flo Waters! What are you doing here?" yelled Hodges.

"I could ask you the same thing," I shouted. "In fact, I will. What are you doing here?"

"Well, I can hardly play *Star Smasher* since you got me banned," he said.

"You got yourself banned," I corrected. Hodges had single-handedly ruined *Star Smasher*, my favourite game and the first one we jumped into, under an alter ego called the Red Ghost. Through a combination of bullying and cheating he had turned a fun game into a miserable experience for everyone else. Fortunately Mum had managed to disable his custom-built hacks and get him permabanned from the game. She had even administered some old-school real-world justice.

"I wasn't allowed to play ANY games thanks to your mum telling my mum everything," he whined. "That was the worst four hours of my life."

I rolled my eyes so hard they almost blew holes in the roof. "You were only banned for four hours?" I asked. "After hacking a game and ruining it for all the other players?"

"And not only that," he said. "I'm not allowed to stream any more. So now I just have to play games with no one else watching. It's unnatural."

"Oh, you poor thing," I said, shaking my head.

"Anyway," he said, "I'm glad I ran into you."

I crept out from behind the bed and headed slowly towards the open door, my laser pistol at the ready. "Yeah, I'll bet you are."

"Is your friend with you?" he asked. "Mike, was it?"

"Max, actually," said Max. "And yes, I'm here."

"Good, it's better if you're both here," said Hodges.

"If you think you're going to take us, you're in for a big disappointment," I said. "We beat you last time and we'll beat you again."

"Yeah, we're heavily armed," threatened Max, gripping his mug furiously as he peered round the side of the bed.

"I wouldn't exactly say you beat me," said Hodges. "I mean, there was some strange stuff going on in that game… But it doesn't matter, that's not what I meant. I wanted to apologize to you."

Max and I scowled. "You want to what?" I demanded, pressing myself up against the wall next to the door so that Hodges and I were inches away from each other.

"Apologize," he repeated. "Four hours without video games is a long time, you know—"

"It's really not," I said.

"Definitely not," agreed Max.

"—And I spent that time reflecting on who I'd let down with my actions."

"The other players?" asked Max.

"The people who watched your streams?" I asked. "Us? Your family?"

"Um … sure," said Hodges. "All those. But mainly myself."

"Right," I said, rolling my eyes again.

Hodges continued, "I mean, some of my behaviour was not very … sportsmanlike."

"You mean the bullying?" I asked, motioning to Max to come over.

Hodges coughed. "Well … yes."

"And the hacking?" asked Max, before tiptoeing across the room.

"Yes, that too," said Hodges.

"And don't forget the

… SNEAK ATTACKS!" I yelled, diving through the doorway and firing into the corridor. But Hodges wasn't there and an innocent vase exploded instead.

"I suppose I was quite sneaky at times, wasn't I?" said Hodges.

Max nervously poked his head out into the corridor. I pointed towards the room at the far end, where Hodges' voice was now coming from. The bathroom. He was cornered.

"I also got to thinking," he continued, "why am I bothering with all these hacks? It's not like I need them. I'm a brilliant gamer without them. What I should really be doing is surrounding myself with players as good as me. Or nearly as good as me. And that's when I thought of you, Waters."

"Nearly as good!" I snapped. "Hodges, I'm twice the gamer you are. Ten times even. A hundred times!"

"Let's not get carried away," said Hodges. "But you've got skills, I'll give you that. You're definitely the best I've played against. Your friend had some pretty sick moves too, if I remember correctly – I still can't figure out how he managed to disarm me in *Star Smasher*. And that's why we should team up."

I almost choked. "Team up? Are you serious?"

"Why not?" he said. "You're good. I'm great. We could dominate this game. Not just this game. Every game. Side by side. What do you say?"

"I say I don't trust you as far as I could throw you," I said, rushing towards the bathroom door. I burst through it and unloaded another charge, destroying the bath, sink and toilet bowl. But again, there was no Hodges.

"He went out the window," I said, pointing at the smashed pane as Max joined me. "Ugh. And now I'm out of charge."

Max seemed a little agitated, hopping from one foot to another. He had the look he gets when he wants to tell me something but knows I'm not going to like it.

"What is it?" I asked.

"Well…" he said, squirming. "Do you think … maybe … I don't know … we should … um … take Hodges up on his offer?"

I squinted at Max, taking in the words he had just said like they were Tetris pieces – my mind desperately trying to fit them together in a way that made sense.

"Sorry … what?" I asked, unable to make the

pieces line up.

"I mean, obviously I'm not Hodges' biggest fan," said Max. "He did shoot me the last time we met. But it's just… This game is about survival, right? Making difficult decisions? All I know is that it's you, me and your mum against ninety-seven other players, and one of the best gamers in the world is offering to team up with us."

"It's a trick," I said. "It has to be, Max. We can't trust him. And besides, he's gone now."

CREAK!

Hodges.

"He must have realized I was out of charge," I said. "He'll be coming back to finish us off."

"Should we jump out of the window?" asked Max.

"No point, he's too good a shot," I said. "Hand me that mug."

"You said it was useless," replied Max.

"It is, but that doesn't mean I won't chuck it at Hodges," I said.

Max handed me the mug and I walked to the top of the stairs.

But it wasn't Hodges. Another player with pink hair and a unicorn horn was waiting for us.

"Oh dear," she said. "Game over for you, sweetie."

I closed my eyes and hurled the mug at her.

After a couple of seconds I opened one eye, then the other. The girl was gone and in her place was Hodges.

"See, we make the perfect team!" Hodges laughed. "You distract them by throwing crockery and then I blast them for the win. It's the perfect combination." He held up his hands. "Look, I know you don't trust me," he said, "and I don't blame you, but think about it. You're unarmed right now – no charge and no mugs. If I wanted to beat you all I would need to do is pull the trigger."

Then, instead of firing, Hodges did something unexpected. He threw the laser cannon down at my feet. I stared at it for a moment, wondering what the trap could be. When nothing obvious sprang to mind I reached for the weapon and pointed it at Hodges.

"Flo, no!" said Max. "You can't, he's unarmed."

"Not really how the game works, Max," I said.

"But he's right," said Max. "He could have killed you but he didn't. We need him."

I pointed the weapon at Hodges for a few more seconds, then let out a groan. I hated it when Max was right. "Fine," I said. "We'll team up, but just this once."

"Great!" said Hodges. "I'll send you a Party-Up request."

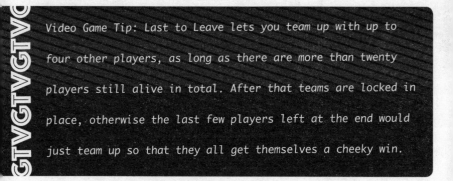

Video Game Tip: Last to Leave lets you team up with up to four other players, as long as there are more than twenty players still alive in total. After that teams are locked in place, otherwise the last few players left at the end would just team up so that they all get themselves a cheeky win.

The following message appeared on our watches:

RED GHOST HAS REQUESTED A PARTY-UP!

(ACCEPT)(DECLINE)

Max and I tapped the 'Accept' button.

"You won't regret this!" said Hodges.

"Already do," I said. I held up the laser cannon.
"I'm keeping this, by the way."

"Hey, who's this other player?" asked Hodges. "I
can see us paired with them on the map."

"That's Flo's mum," said Max. "We need to get to
the Arctic Zone to save her."

"Riiiight," said Hodges, turning to me. "So … do
you always play video games with your mum now?"

"Not always," I said. "Just a surprising number of
times when you're in the same game as us. Anyway,
we need to find some wheels, it's too far to walk."

"Hmm," said Hodges. "I might have a solution.
But it doesn't involve wheels as such…"

LEVEL 4

Hodges had led us out of the house and across a few streets until we reached a narrow river, where we found a speedboat waiting for us. Now we were shooting up the river, heading north towards the Arctic Zone. It was AMAZING.

"WOOOOO HOOOOO!"

"Are you sure you don't want me to drive?" asked Hodges.

I gave him a stern look. "I said no."

"All right," he sighed. "I mean, I did find us the boat but whatever. Just let me know if you want me to take over. Driving is one of my gaming specialties."

"Too bad keeping quiet isn't another. I need to concentrate," I said as the river suddenly widened, going from maybe ten metres across to more like a thousand.

"Hey, look what I found in the back of the boat," said Max, holding up a pair of binoculars.

"Nice one, Max," I said. "Use them to look along the coast, see if there's any sign of Mum."

Max glanced at his watch. "According to the map the other team should be coming up alongside the riverbank any moment now," he said. He held the binoculars up to his eyes.

"We seem to be going to a lot of effort to rescue your mum," noted Hodges. "Wouldn't it be easier just to quit and start another game? I mean, no offence, but from what I remember of your mum in *Star Smasher*, she wasn't exactly the best player I've ever seen. More like the worst…"

"If you want to leave, leave," I said. "But we're staying and winning this one."

"You don't give up easily, do you?" he asked.

"Not if I can help it," I said.

Max pointed towards the shore. "There's the truck," he said. "And I can see your mum. She looks OK. Confused but OK. It doesn't seem like the other team have seen her yet."

"So now what?" asked Hodges.

"Now we save her," I said.

"How, exactly?" he persisted. "We have one blaster between the three of us, unless you've got something else you haven't told me about."

"Nope," said Max. "Just a clock."

Hodges frowned. "A clock?" he asked. "But there aren't any clo—"

"Leave getting Mum back to me," I interrupted, turning the boat towards the truck.

The other team may not have seen Mum yet, but it wasn't long before they spotted us. We could tell by the multiple laser blasts they started firing our way.

A plan began to form in my head. I wouldn't exactly call it a safe plan, or even a smart one. It was the kind of plan that wasn't worth suggesting, because the others would only scream and shout and try to talk me out of it. But I knew it was our only option.

"We're getting too close," yelled Hodges.

"Not close enough," I corrected, pushing the boat even further towards the shore so that we were practically riding alongside the truck. Snow was starting to fall now, meaning we were entering the Arctic Zone. Laser blasts kept narrowly missing us, stray shots skipping off the water like pebbles.

"Flo, you're going to get us killed!" shouted Max.

"Mack's right," agreed Hodges. "We're about two seconds away from being blown to smithereens."

"It's Max, not Mack!" yelled Max.

"Hold on to something," I said, pushing the accelerator as far down as it would go. The boat crept ahead of the truck. I was only going to get one shot at this, so it had to be perfect. "Just a little bit more…"

"FLO! FLO!"

I glanced to my left. Mum had stood up and was waving at us.

"FLO! IT'S ME – YOUR MUM!"

"Mum, no, get back down!" I yelled, but it was too late. The two players in the back of the truck had heard her and were readying their weapons. There was no more time. It had to be now.

Without warning, I spun the wheel round, causing us to almost tip over as we turned. Before the others realized what was happening, the boat hit the shore, the underside slamming into a rock and launching us into the air.

The next few seconds seemed to pass in slow motion.

As the truck continued forwards, the boat crossed

its path a few metres above the ground, spinning in mid-air. At the moment we were directly over the truck, the boat was entirely upside down.

With one hand firmly on the wheel I leaned out, grabbing hold of Mum's arm and pulling her with us as the boat spun back round and crashed into the snow on the far side of the road.

Of course, the biggest problem with heroically corkscrewing a boat on to land is that afterwards the boat is pretty much done as a means of transportation. Unlike the truck, which had skidded to an abrupt stop just a dozen metres or so from us.

"Flo, I…" began Mum.

All I wanted to do was hug her but I knew we had to move. "Hold that thought, Mum," I said. As the four of us clambered out of the boat, the truck started to turn back towards us.

"Why didn't you tell us you were going to do that?" shouted Max.

"Because you would have said no," I retorted.
"But we haven't really got time to go into that now.
Speaking of time, could you give me that clock,
Max?"

"The clock?" he said. "Why do you want that?"

"Probably because it's not a clock," said Hodges.

Max looked confused. "What do you mean it's
not a clock?" he asked. "It's got a clock face on it,
what else would it be?"

"Think about it, Mitch," said Hodges.

"It's Max, not Mitch," said Max. "And the only
other thing I can think of that might have a clock
face on it would be a … oh. Oh no. Flo, please
don't tell me I've been carrying around a bomb
thinking it was a harmless clock."

"This is exactly why I didn't tell you, Max," I said.
"Because I knew you'd get worried. Now can I

please have it? It's quite important –
that truck is almost here."

Max started patting himself down,
frantically searching for the bomb.
"I really wish you wouldn't make
decisions for other people all the
time, Flo," he said. "It's really rude
and … and… That's odd. I don't
have it any more."

My eyes went wide. "What do
you mean you don't have it?" I
asked, grabbing him by the shoulders.

"I don't know," he said. "I had it in the boat.
And then you flipped the boat and it must
have fallen out."

"It fell out … when I flipped the boat?" I said,
turning back to the truck. "I wonder i—"

KA-BOOOOOOMMMM!

Crates and various
pieces of truck went flying
everywhere, landing all around us.

"Well," I said as we stared at the wreckage.

"I suppose that will do."

LEVEL 5

"Mum!" I yelled, throwing my arms round her.

"Flo!" she said, squeezing me tight. "And Max!"

Mum grabbed Max and almost smothered him with her arms.

"Hi, Ms Waters," he said.

"When did they add a hug emote?" asked Hodges.

Video Game Tip: Emotes are actions you can perform to express yourself in games, typically the sort of thing you'd do in everyday life, like giving someone a thumbs up, pulling a funny face or performing an overly complicated breakdancing routine.

"It's … uh … premium content," I said. "You've got to pay for it."

"Cool, I'll have to buy it later," he said. "That reminds me, I just bought a new Irish-dancing emote. Check it out."

Mum, Max and I watched with bemusement and, in my case at least, horror as Hodges proceeded to prance about in the snow with his arms fixed to his sides.

"Er … thanks for that," I said when he was finally done.

"Flo, sweetheart, we need to talk," said Mum.

"Yeah, we do, but not now," I said, and gave Hodges a sideways glance.

"OK," she agreed. "And those people who were in the truck—"

I waved her away. "Don't worry about them," I said. "They'll probably already be in another game by now."

"I'm not so sure," said Mum, pointing behind us. Max, Hodges and I turned to see the four players emerging from behind the wreckage of the truck.

"They must have jumped off at the last second!" I said. "Don't worry though, this time they're about to come up against Flo Waters WITH a laser cannon."

I brought the laser cannon up, picked out a target and pulled the trigger.

Nothing happened.

"Um … yeah … about that," said Hodges.

"Hodges," I said calmly. "This laser cannon, the one you handed to me. The one you gave to me as sign of peace. It wouldn't happen to have been empty all along, would it?"

"A little bit," admitted Hodges.

"ARGH! What is wrong with you?" I shouted.

"You might have actually shot me!" he said. "And in my defence, I did use the last of the charge saving you."

"What's our plan now?" asked Max.

"Now?" I said. "Now we RUN!"

The four of us sprinted away across the snowy fields. As stray laser blasts whizzed past our heads, I knew we'd have to find a hiding place soon, preferably somewhere that also had some new equipment we could use to defend ourselves. But the frozen landscape wasn't exactly presenting us with many possibilities. The one plus was the ever-worsening snowstorm, which would give us some cover from our attackers, but there was no telling how long that would last. I could just about make out some industrial-looking buildings through the blizzard but they seemed a long way off. We needed to find something closer.

"Follow me," yelled Hodges through the snow.

"Where to?" I shouted back.

"Trust me," he said.

"After what you pulled with the laser cannon?" I said.

"Are you still going on about that?" he said.

"It was two minutes ago!" I yelled.

"Annoying, huh?" said Max.

"Yes!" I said.

"Don't worry, you get used to it after a while," he replied.

I had no idea what he was talking about. He barely knew Hodges.

"Come on," said Hodges. "I know where we might be able to lose them."

Without waiting for my reply Hodges continued onwards into the snowstorm. Max and Mum followed swiftly behind him, leaving me with no choice but to join them.

After running for about a minute we came to the edge of a cliff. But rather than turn round, Hodges hopped off it.

"Did that boy just jump off a cliff?" asked Mum.

"I think he did," said Max.

The three of us peered over the edge. Below us, standing on a narrow ledge that jutted from the rock a little way down, was Hodges.

"Hurry up!" he shouted, before somehow vanishing into the rock itself.

"Did that boy just walk through a cliff?" asked Mum.

"I think he did," said Max. "Come on," I said. One by one we dropped down on to the ledge. Behind us was the entrance to a cave. We rushed inside to find a sprawling cavern of ice.

"Not bad, eh?" said Hodges. "Hardly anyone knows about this place because it's so well hidden."

The ice cave looked like it had been decorated by a supervillain plotting to blow up the planet. There were metal walkways, banks of old-fashioned computer terminals and flashing buttons everywhere. Clearly no other players had found this spot yet as the place was littered with good loot.

"I think now would probably be a good time to find some gear," I said. "Let's split into two groups. Me, Max and Mum in one and Hodges in the other."

"Not exactly even, is it?" said Hodges.

"I'm sure you'll manage," I said.

"You're not planning on ditching me are you, Waters?" he asked.

"No," I said. "And even if I was, we're paired up. You could see us on the map."

"You can still kick me out of the party," he said. "Up until the last twenty players, remember."

"Hmm, tempting," I said. "But no, we're not going to ditch you. Just go find some equipment."

"Fine," grumbled Hodges, wandering off deeper into the cave.

When I was sure he was out of earshot, I turned to Mum. "What are you doing here?"

Mum looked confused. "I thought we were about to start looking for equipment?"

"I think Flo meant why are you in the game," explained Max.

"Oh," said Mum. "That. I've been trying to get you both out of the games, you see. My first attempt back in *Star Smasher* obviously didn't work out.

Instead of coming back to the real world you jumped into another game, *Blocktopia*. I tried to join that one but it's not multiplayer."

While Mum talked I started picking up nearby items, including a helmet, some medical supplies and, thankfully, some charge for the laser cannon. "But you were there in the last game, right?" I said. "*Critter Clash*?"

"In a way," she said. "It turns out the version you were playing was quite out of date. Which was lucky, because after doing some digging I discovered that version had a number of bugs and security holes in it. All things they've fixed in later versions of course, but I was able to exploit those holes and insert my own code into the game."

"That's what allowed you to control those shape-shifting monsters?" asked Max. "And send us messages?"

"Exactly," she said. "Although that wasn't my first plan. I had inserted what I hoped would be a portal that would let you escape the game. Unfortunately I placed it inside the stomach of a small rabbit. The only way I could find of directing you to its location involved hijacking two of the characters to send you messages. Still, it worked out in the end."

Max and I looked at each other. "No, it didn't," I said. "We're still here!"

"Yes, fine, if you're going to be picky," said Mum, folding her arms. "The portal didn't quite work. However, I had a backup plan. This one will definitely work – I'm one hundred per cent sure this time. I've written a very complicated new program that will extract us from the game provided we execute the necessary software trigger."

"Mum – in English, please!" I said.

"We need to win the game, dear," she said. "Unfortunately, the only way to upload my program was for someone to reactivate the device that got you in here in the first place. I had no choice but to enter the game with you."

"And you're really sure winning will work this time?" Max asked.

"Oh yes," she said. "Ninety-five per cent."

"You said one hundred a second ago," I said.

"Did I?" she said. "Well, I meant ninety-five. Ninety, tops."

"What are you guys talking about?" asked Hodges, reappearing behind us and making me jump. "Not plotting behind my back, I hope?"

"Don't sneak up on people like that!" I said. "And um … nothing… We were just talking about…"

Hodges' avatar narrowed his eyes and rubbed his chin thoughtfully.

"Don't use the suspicion emote on me," I said. "Why are you back so soon anyway?"

"Haven't you seen the map?" he asked.

"No, why?" I replied, tapping my watch. The map hologram appeared and I immediately saw what he meant.

"Why is the map shrinking?" asked Max, waving at the edges of the playing area.

"It's the Void," I said quietly. "It's coming."

LEVEL 6

"What's the Void?" asked Mum.

"The Void is the space where the map used to be," said Hodges.

"Every so often the playing area shrinks," I explained, pointing to a section of the map. "You see how there's this big square? That's the current safe zone. In a few minutes everything outside it will be gone, lost to the Void."

"But … we're not in the safe zone," said a panicked Max.

"Exactly," I said. "We need to clear out of here."

"Good job some of us bothered to find some gear," said Hodges, dropping a variety of weapons and equipment.

Mum, Max and I exchanged sheepish glances. "Er … yeah, good work, Hodges," I said. "Not much luck here, unfortunately."

"Right," said Hodges, sounding unconvinced.

Mum, Max and I quickly stocked up. I made sure to grab a laser cannon and laser pistol, plenty of charge, some health packs and an armoured vest and helmet. I handed Mum and Max two blasters, but knowing they'd never hit anything with them I slipped the charges out beforehand. They'd feel safer with the pistols but, as I was a much better shot, they'd actually be safer if I had enough charge to protect them.

We rushed through the cave after Hodges,

scurrying along the metal gangways, over frozen pipes and along hollowed-out tunnels in the ice until finally emerging into the open air. The snow had stopped falling but in the near distance we could see the Void approaching fast, destroying everything in its path. Unbelievably though, that wasn't our biggest problem.

"It's that other team again!" Hodges shouted.

He gestured at the four players we'd lost when we jumped into the cave. They were running towards us, or more accurately, running away from the Void. Suddenly though, they changed direction, turning left.

"Where are they going?" asked Max.

"There!" I yelled, pointing at two snow speeders that looked to be about the same distance from us as from the other team. "Come on, before they get to them!"

The four of us sprinted across the field while the other team did the same. It was going to be close. Clearly too close for the other team's liking as the four of them stopped running and started firing at us instead.

"Don't stop!" I yelled as the blasts whizzed past us. "They can't shoot and run at the same time."

It was a huge gamble but it worked. Two laser blasts

struck me on the way, one on the arm and one on the leg, but it wasn't enough to stop me reaching the first of the speeders. "Mum, get on," I yelled. "Max, you go with Hodges."

I turned the ignition on the handlebar and the vehicle shot off. Seconds later I heard the sound of the second one behind me. I looked back as the other team unloaded shot after shot at us. Moments later the Void was upon them and the shots stopped coming.

We travelled in silence after that, mainly because of the concentration required to avoid accidentally hitting a stray log or a bush and flipping over. We had to be careful not to do any more damage before we had a chance to use some of the health packs Hodges had found. We also needed to keep a lookout for any other teams. The speeders were great at travelling large distances quickly but they came at a price. They were extremely noisy and anyone nearby would definitely hear us coming.

As if to prove my point, a blast struck the front of my speeder just as we approached the Jungle Zone.

"Argh, hold on," I yelled to Mum as the vehicle skidded out of control, sliding over the last of the snow and coming to a halt in the thick green jungle grass.

Video Game Tip: While in the real world it would be quite unusual, and even worrying, to go from one ecosystem like a snowy wilderness to an exotic jungle in a single step, in video games it's fine.

As Mum and I scrambled to our feet, Hodges and Max pulled up alongside us. We took cover behind some trees as more shots whizzed past.

"It's coming from the forest," said Hodges.

"Well, if they wanted to mess with me, they should have done it before I had a laser cannon," I said.

"I don't feel that great," said Max.

"Me neither," said Mum. "I think some of the lasers back there hit us."

"You and Mum use some of the health packs to heal up here," I said, taking one myself. "Hodges and I will take out those other players."

"We will?" asked Hodges.

"Yeah," I said, feeling my health regenerating. "Unless you want me to do it myself?"

"No, no, I'll help!" he said.

"Just try not to shoot me," I said.

"What if someone shows up while you're gone?" asked Max.

"Then shout for us," I said. "And you've both got laser pistols. Just point and shoot. But we'll be back before then, don't worry."

Hodges and I left Max and Mum and cautiously headed further into the jungle, using the thick trees for cover. It was quiet. I checked the map and the Void had stopped moving, so it was unlikely the other players had retreated, knowing we were here. More likely they were moving into a better position and hoping to—

ZZAPPP!

—ambush us! The blast only just missed.

"Up there!" shouted Hodges, returning fire into the branches of a tree. Moments later a man wearing a baseball cap and a leather jacket dropped out of the tree, landing with a splat on the jungle floor.

"Watch out," I yelled, ducking under another blast, this one coming from behind a nearby rock.

Rather than hide, I ran towards the attacker, hopped on to the rock and then somersaulted over the player, blasting her in mid-air.

"Nice!" said Hodges. "Look, two more over there."

We took aim and fired as two players dressed as ninjas came running towards us. They both dropped at the same time and all four team members vanished.

"We took out the whole team," said Hodges. "At least I think it was just the one team."

"Think again," said another voice. A boy dressed as a pirate stepped in front of us, holding a laser pistol in each hand. One pistol was pointed at Hodges, the other at me. And the boy wasn't alone. Three more pirates appeared, the four of them surrounding us.

I could see Hodges' avatar looking around and knew we were thinking the same thing. Between us we could handle two of them but the other two would take us out. The other team would know this as well. They'd also know that the players left standing would be able to revive their teammates.

Video Game Tip: In Battle Royale games it's possible to revive downed teammates. You will have a limited time to do this. It can also leave you vulnerable to attack and your teammate will only have a small amount of health when they come back, but if you don't do it, they'll almost certainly moan at you about it. A lot. If all the members of a team are downed, then it's game over for that team.

What they didn't know was at that very second a massive wrecking ball was swinging towards them.

They quickly found out though. It smashed straight through two of the pirates, leaving the other two – and Hodges and myself – stunned. Fortunately, we reacted first, blasting the remaining pirates.

"Where did that come from?" asked Hodges as the wrecking ball swung back and forth.

We stared up into the branches as a rope ladder dropped to the ground.

"Up here!" shouted Max as he and Mum looked down on us from a wooden platform high in the trees, both of them grinning from ear to ear.

LEVEL 7

Hodges and I quickly climbed the rope ladder,
Mum and Max helping pull us up on to the wooden
platform. Behind the platform was a treehouse – a
wooden cabin with windows facing out in every
direction. As we stepped inside I could see that it
would be the perfect hideout until we had to move
on again.

"How did you find this?" I asked them.

"Find it?" asked Mum. "We didn't find it, dear. We
built it."

"You didn't tell us this game had a crafting

element to it," said Max, sounding a little annoyed. Max loved games that let you build stuff. Me, not so much.

"To be honest, I forgot," I admitted.

"I didn't even know," said Hodges. "But then I tend to think, why build something when you could blow it up instead?"

"Exactly!" I said. "That's a very good way of putting it."

Max rolled his eyes. "Anyway, after you left we realized we could convert things like trees, plants and rocks to building materials so we quickly threw together this treehouse. Sorry it's a bit rough, we didn't have much time."

"Right," I said, not bothering to point out the chandelier hanging from the ceiling or the welcome mat at the door. "And the wrecking ball?"

"That was me," said Mum. "I spotted you were in trouble. Once Max had kindly showed me how to create materials, I made a rope and a giant cement ball. Physics took care of the rest."

Hodges put his arm round Max and me. "What a great team we make," he said. "Everyone doing their bit. We're unstoppable."

"Get off," I said, pushing his arm away. "Don't get cocky. There's still a long way to go before we win. And just so we're absolutely clear – we have to win this game."

Hodges nodded approvingly. "It's not often I find someone who needs to win as much as I do. Have you considered … you know?"

"You know … what?" I asked, narrowing my eyes.

Hodges grinned knowingly. "I mean, back in *Star Smasher*, your mum managed to stop my hacks in minutes. I'm sure she must have a few tricks up her sleeve she can use for this game."

"Oh no, I don't think—" began Mum.

"We don't cheat!" I interrupted.

"OK, OK," said Hodges, holding up his hands. "I just meant that since winning this game seems so important to you…"

"It is important to *us*," I said. "But that doesn't mean we're going to cheat. Ugh, why would I expect you to understand? All you've ever known is cheating to win games."

"That's not true!" protested Hodges. "I'm a great gamer. I just got carried away with winning. Haven't you ever made mistakes?"

"No, never," I said.

Mum and Max stared at me with raised eyebrows.

"Well … maybe once or twice," I mumbled.

"But I'm a lot more trustworthy than you."

"Is that so?" said Hodges. "Like when you told your best friend he was carrying a clock instead of a bomb?"

"That was different," I said. "I was trying to protect him."

"Oh, OK," said Hodges. "And I suppose you were trying to protect him by leaving him and your mum with zero charge in their laser pistols. Yeah, that's right, I saw you slip out their charges before we left."

Max rounded on me. "What? You left us unarmed?"

"I–I–I just thought I could put the charge to better use," I said. "You were quite safe. I would have been back at the first sign of any danger."

"I'm not a coward, Flo," said Max.

"I know—" I said.

"Then stop treating me like one!" said Max.

"Flo?" said Mum. I should have known she would have something to say here.

"Please, Mum," I said. "Can you not lecture me too?"

Mum shook her head. "I was just going to say—"

"What? That I should trust people more? That I should stop always trying to do everything by myself? That there's no I in team?"

Mum folded her arms. "Well, yes, all those things are true, Flo. But what I'm trying to tell you is that huge black wall thing is heading our way again."

"Oh," I said quietly. "Right. We'd better go then."

"I think so, yes," said Mum.

I brought up the map using my watch. "All right, it looks like the safe area is moving east. My guess is it's heading to the Grasslands, so we'll have to go through the Desert Zone first. I mean, if that's OK with everyone else."

The others nodded and mumbled in agreement. There was a lot of tension in the treehouse and, weirdly, hardly any of it was due to the Void.

"Down the rope ladder then. Let's go," I said.

Max had just started climbing down when Hodges grabbed him by the arm.

"Hey, what are you doing?" I demanded.

"Look!" said Hodges, pointing towards the ground. I could just make out the shapes of what had to be players running across the jungle floor.

"If we go down there now, we'll run right into them," he said as he pulled Max back up.

"If we don't then the Void will get us," I said, looking around. "Unless…"

I reached out and grabbed a vine that was hanging from a tree.

"You can't be serious," said Max.

"What's wrong?" I grinned. "Too scary?"

Max opened his mouth to speak, then let out a sigh. The four of us each grabbed on to a vine, took a deep breath, then jumped.

"ARRRRGGGGHHHHH!!!"

screamed Max as we swung through the jungle.

It was more or less the same noise as Mum and I were making. Hodges was the only exception since his avatar was swinging while he himself sat in the comfort of his bedroom.

"You three really get into your games," he observed when we landed on the edge of the jungle, next to the Desert Zone.

"If you only knew," muttered Max. "Hey, look, there's a car over there."

Sure enough there was an old, beat-up hatchback parked on the sand not too far from us.

"Ow!" cried Max as a laser bolt struck him on the arm.

Suddenly we were under attack again, the blasts coming from the jungle behind us. "Return fire," I shouted, aiming back into the trees.

"We don't have charge, remember?" yelled Max.

"Get to the car then," I said.

As Max and Mum sprinted to the vehicle, Hodges and I aimed our pistols towards our attackers. I quickly took out an elderly lady with a Mohawk hairstyle who was hiding behind a bush and Hodges made short work of a man dressed in a tiger suit.

"How many were there?" asked Hodges.

"Three, I think," I said.

"I don't see anyone else," he said, stepping slowly into the forest.

Suddenly, out of the corner of my eye I spotted something running towards Hodges. Instinctively I spun round and fired off a dozen shots.

"I got him," I said, pointing towards a man dressed in a superhero costume who quickly vanished, meaning his entire squad was out of action.

But that wasn't all I had hit.

Hodges was lying face down on the ground.

"You shot me!" he shouted.

"It was an accident," I said.

"Sure it was," he said sarcastically as Max and Mum pulled up in the car, Mum at the wheel. Max hopped out.

"Flo, what did you do?" asked Max.

"Relax, it was just a bit of friendly fire," I said.

Max kneeled down and put a hand on Hodges' back. The two of them jolted as if they'd had a static shock.

"What was that?" asked Max.

"You're reviving him," I said. "See, no harm done."

Max held his hand in place and sure enough in a few seconds' time Hodges was standing upright again.

"Let's get going," I said, climbing into the car. Max

followed but Hodges stayed where he was.

"Come on, Hodges," I said.

"I'm not coming with you," he replied firmly.

I rolled my eyes. "It was an accident. I said I was sorry."

"No, you didn't!"

"Pretty sure I did," I said, though truthfully I couldn't remember if I had.

"You don't trust me," said Hodges. "And now I'm pretty sure I don't trust you. I'll find my own way to the safe zone."

"Don't be daft, Hodges," I shouted. "I trust you, all right? Let's go."

"You're lying," he said. "If you trust me then tell me why it's so important for you to win this one game?"

"I … well… It doesn't matter, we just do," I said.

"Flo, maybe we should just tell him," said Max.

"No!" I hissed.

"That's what I thought," said Hodges. He turned and ran, heading south west.

"Now what?" asked Max.

"Leave him," I said. "Let's go."

LEVEL 8

"Can you believe Hodges?" I asked as the car bounced across the sand dunes. Normally I would insist on driving in video games but I was so mad I thought it best to let Mum take the wheel.

"You did shoot him, dear," said Mum.

"And you clearly don't trust him," said Max. "At all."

"Whose side are you on?" I asked.

"We're on yours, Flo," said Max. "But so is Hodges."

Our watches made a little ping sound and a notification hologram appeared in front of us.

RED GHOST HAS LEFT THE TEAM!

"Not any more he's not," I sighed. I tapped the watch again to bring up the game stats screen. "There are twenty-nine players left. Nine to go, then the teams are locked until the end."

"Um … Flo," said Mum, looking in the rear-view mirror. "I think most of those players might be behind us right now."

She was right. There were at least five vehicles on our tail – two motorbikes, a 4x4, an open-top sports car and…

"Is that an ice-cream van?" asked Max.

"This is a very silly game," said Mum.

"They're trying to get to the safe zone," I said.
"Not if I can help it though."

"We can help too," said Max.

"Right, right," I said, reloading my laser cannon.
I took some spare charge and handed it to him.

"No, you keep that," he said. "I've still got building
materials that your mum and I picked up earlier.
I can help in my own way."

I nodded, slipping the charge back into my pocket. One of the motorbikes appeared on our left, with two chiselled bodybuilder guys riding it – one driving and one carrying a bazooka. On the other side of the car, the second motorbike pulled up, with just one rider on it.

As bazooka guy started loading his weapon, I fired blasts at him, but his driver was annoyingly good, weaving in and out of my shots, keeping his partner protected. The bazooka loaded, the passenger took aim.

Max threw himself down on to the back seat of the car as a rocket fired through one window and out through Max's. It struck the other bike, causing what some might say was an over-the-top explosion. Normally such things made me deliriously happy, but not today. Something was still bugging me.

"You know, you didn't help with Hodges," I said, pointing my laser cannon at the car door. "You were about to tell him about us being stuck in the game."

I fired a blast, knocking the door off and sending it spinning through the air until it crashed into bazooka guy and his friend, causing another arguably overblown explosion.

"Good shot," said Max. "Would it have been so bad to tell Hodges the truth?"

"Yes!" I said, looking out at the convertible that had moved into position right behind us. I climbed out of the window of our car and on to the roof. Max opened his door and I pulled him up.

"OK, no need to panic," Mum was muttering to herself. "My daughter and her friend are standing on top of the car now. And I'm driving. This is perfectly normal."

"Hodges might have been able to help somehow," said Max. "He's good with computers."

"We've got Mum for that," I said, flinging myself off the roof and landing in the passenger seat of the convertible. "Hey," I said to the driver, a girl dressed as a sailor.

"Ugh, get out!" she demanded.

I didn't get out. Instead I put my hands in front of her eyes.

"Stop that! I can't see," she said.

"Look out for the rock," I said.

"Where? WHERE? MOVE YOUR HANDS!" she cried as she turned the wheel left and right trying to avoid the rock.

I took my hands away. "There," I said, pointing at a massive stone in the road. I jumped out as the car struck the rock, the explosion propelling me into the air where I grabbed hold of the crane that was now attached to our car.

"Sorry it's a bit slapdash," said Max. "If I'd had more time to build it…"

"It's perfect," I said, hanging on with both arms as we continued to race across the desert. "As I was saying, Mum has all the computing knowledge we need. I've got total confidence in her. She's ninety per cent sure her plan is going to work and that's good enough for me."

"Maybe more like eighty per cent," said Mum. "Call it seventy to be safe."

"Seventy per cent?" I repeated. "But you said… Oh, it doesn't matter. The point is that we'll be out of the game soon enough. We can't risk letting someone else know that we're stuck here. If he actually believes us, just think about the danger that puts us in."

"You're literally dangling from a crane attached to a car going about eighty miles an hour across a desert while being chased by vehicles driven by armed players shooting lasers at you!" shouted Max. "HOW MUCH MORE DANGER COULD YOU POSSIBLY BE IN?"

Typical Max overreacting. I wasn't in that much danger.

At that point a cactus struck me, sending me tumbling through the air.

"FLO!" yelled Max and Mum in unison.

As I spun backwards I reached out and felt my fingers grasp something.

Something large. And pink. With sprinkles.

I was holding on to the giant strawberry ice-cream cone that was fixed to the top of the ice-cream van. Meanwhile the driver – a woman dressed as a princess with a strawberry dress and a tiara – tried to hit me with lasers as she drove.

Fine, NOW I was in danger.

"Hold on, sweetheart!" yelled Mum. I looked down as our car fell back alongside the van. My first thought was to jump but it was a risk – a very splatty kind of risk.

Max swung the crane round towards me. It didn't quite reach the cone but I figured with a good kick-off I might make—

"LOOK OUT!" I yelled as the 4x4 moved into position on the other side of our car, before proceeding to ram into it, creating a deafening bang. Sparks flew from the car and it wobbled and skidded a little, but Mum somehow kept control and Max managed to hold on to the crane on the roof. The 4x4 turned away from the car but then came back even harder, smashing once more into Mum's side. This time the force almost knocked Max off the car and Mum struggled to keep us from spinning out of control. The 4x4 started moving out again and I knew there was no way the car would withstand a third blow.

Max was leaning down through the window, talking to Mum. I couldn't hear what they said but I saw Mum give him a nod.

The 4x4 came roaring towards us but just as they were about to collide, Mum hammered the brake and the car seemed to shoot backwards. The 4x4 however kept going and crashed into the ice-cream van instead. The van couldn't cope with being rammed the way the car had. It lost its balance immediately, tipping over. But it didn't quite go down without a fight, as the impact caused the 4x4 to flip over as well. And me? Well, things didn't go great for me either.

I was sent flying into the air, practically back-flipping over the van and 4x4 as they exploded beneath me. As I hurtled towards the ground, I thought two things:

1. What a cool way to go out, and
2. **AAARRRGHHHHH!!!!**

And then, as I was about to hit the ground, the crane on the top of the car swung round with Max dangling off it by one hand, snatching me out of the air with the other.

The car came to a stop a few metres from the end of the Desert Zone, where the Grasslands began. Max let me down, then climbed off himself.

"Told you I'm not a coward," he said.

"That was incredible," I said. "Both of you were amazing."

Mum got out of the car and nodded. "We were a bit, weren't we?" she said, grinning. "Unfortunately that's the car out of fuel, so we'll have to go on foot now."

At that moment, our watches beeped. "It's an alert," I said. "We're down to the final twenty players."

"So Hodges…" said Max.

"He's our enemy now," I said. "Again."

There was a brief silence. Max was right. I should have been more trusting of Hodges. I hadn't trusted Max and Mum to look after themselves and yet they'd had to save me.

"Max," I said. "I should have—"

As I went to finish that thought, there was a movement from the wreckage of the ice-cream van. Out stepped the princess, her strawberry dress now blackened. Before I could react, she fired her laser cannon.

The blast struck Max in the centre of the chest and he dropped to the ground.

LEVEL 9

I returned fire, blasting the princess, who disappeared instantly, which meant there was no one left on her squad to revive her. Max was luckier. Mum had already placed a hand on his back to start the healing process.

In the distance the Void was making its way towards us but a glance at the map confirmed we were safe for now, although there wasn't a lot of playing area left. We were fast approaching the endgame now. The map was reduced to an area of the Grasslands about half a mile wide, at the centre of which was a bridge.

"Thanks, Ms Waters," said Max as he got to his feet.

"Use a health pack to get back to full strength," I said. "Then we need to move. We're way too exposed out here."

Aside from the odd tree, bush or rock, the Grasslands didn't offer much in the way of cover, which made us vulnerable. There were nineteen – no – eighteen players left, so fifteen not including us. Fourteen not including Hodges, if he was still alive. I had a feeling he was.

Max finished healing and we made our way across the field, heading in the general direction of the bridge. We kept ourselves low, constantly looking over our shoulders as we went.

"Max, can I borrow your binoculars, please?" I asked.

Max looked a little surprised.

"What?" I said.

"No, nothing," he said. "It's just I've never heard you use the word 'Please' before."

"I have," said Mum. "But it's usually followed up with 'can I get a new game?'."

"Yeah, yeah, you're both hilarious," I said. "Can I have the binoculars, PLEASE?"

Max handed them over and I did a quick scan around us but couldn't see anyone.

Then a thought occurred to me.

"Mum…" I said.

"Yes, dear?"

"If your plan to get us out of the game doesn't work, what happens after that?"

"Oh, don't worry about that," said Mum, waving me away. "I told you, there's a sixty-five per cent chance it will be fine."

"You started off at a hundred," I said. "Seriously, Mum, if this fails are we just going to keep jumping from video game to video game forever?"

Mum didn't reply at first, instead clearing her throat with a cough. "Um … well, no," she said. "Not forever…"

Max and I stopped walking. "Mum, what do you mean?" I asked.

Mum screwed up her face, the way she did whenever she had to deliver bad news. "Well … when I was investigating how to get you two out, I noticed that the game locker you use – G-Locker – contains tons of games. A lot more than I ever remember buying you, to be perfectly honest, but now isn't the time to go into that. The problem is that you only actually have four of those games currently installed."

I shrugged. "Yeah, of course. No point in taking up space with games you're not playing regularly," I said. And then added, "Oh."

"What does that mean?" asked Max. "Are you saying we've run out of games to jump to?"

Mum shrugged. "Honestly, I don't know," she said. "I figure one of two things can happen. Either we just jump back to the first game and go round again or…"

She didn't have to finish the sentence. We knew what she meant.

"It might be nice to see Gary again," I said, smiling, trying to make light of things.

"Yeah." Max nodded, putting on a brave face. "We

can catch up with Girdy. And Hungrabun and Kiwi."

We looked at Mum.

"It'll be fine," she said. "A sixty per cent chance is still pretty good."

"And what happens if we're hit but we're not revived in time?" asked Max.

"Most likely one of the same options," said Mum. "But hopefully we don't find out."

"If we ever get out of here, I'm going to learn to say 'no' to you, Flo," said Max determinedly. "I wouldn't be here if I'd just learned not to do everything you tell me."

"Max, stop," I said, dropping down. "Both of you, get down."

"OK," he said as he and Mum dived into a patch of long grass. "Oh, now, this is exactly what I'm talking about. You say get down and I do it, just like that."

"There's at least two squads on their way here," I said. "But if now is the time you want to stop listening to me, then…"

"All right, all right," he said.

A two-man squad was approaching from the west while a three-woman squad had arrived from the east. I peered up from the grass and caught the moment when both teams spotted each other. They immediately opened fire, filling the air above us with laser beams.

A couple of stray blasts struck Mum on the head and legs. It was enough to put her out of action.

"Hold on," I said, crawling a few metres over to her. Half a minute later I had revived her and she took a health kit to get herself back to full strength.

"How many of those do we have left?" I asked. "I've only got one."

"Me too," said Max.

"That's me out," said Mum.

"OK," I said. "We need to be extra careful from now on. Keep hidden as best we can and— Oh, come on, Max!"

"Sorry," said Max. Another couple of blasts had taken him out again.

"Mum, you take care of Max and I'll take care of them," I said, tilting my head towards the warring squads.

Crouching in the grass as lasers shot overhead, I took aim at one of the girls in the distance. Then something caught my eye.

"The Void," I said. "It's nearly here."

You'd think a giant wall of darkness would be hard to miss, but both groups were so busy shooting at each other they didn't notice it approaching. And when they finally did spot it, it was too late. The player counter dropped by five in just a few seconds.

Thirteen left.

I stood up. "Let's go. We don't have much time." But for some reason Max was still down. The reason quickly became clear – Mum was down too.

"I think I may have also been hit," said Mum.

"YOU THINK?" I said.

I looked towards the Void. We had about thirty

seconds before it reached us. The game didn't let you revive more than one player at a time and there wasn't going to be time to revive them both.

Mum and Max must have realized the problem too.

"Save your mum," said Max.

"No, Flo, save Max," said Mum.

"That's very brave and noble of you both, but it doesn't exactly help me make the decision," I said.

"It has to be Max," said Mum. "He's better at games than me. You two have a better chance of winning."

"But what about you?" I said. "We can't just leave you. You said it could be the end."

"Or it might not be," she said. "Either way you don't have a choice. Please, Flo, just this once, do what I ask."

I kneeled down beside Max and put a hand on his back. It felt like it was taking longer and longer to heal him while the Void seemed to move faster and faster. All the while my eyes were welling up.

"You'll be OK?" I asked Mum.

"Sure," she smiled. "Fifty-fifty. Love you."

"Love you too," I said.

With the Void barely a metre away, Max finally sprang up. We took one last look at Mum.

"Go," she whispered.

Then we turned and ran.

LEVEL 10

We reached the safe zone and took shelter in a little wooden hut.

Neither of us could speak after what had just happened. There were no words. All we could do was give each other the same look of anguish.

In the end it was Mum who broke the silence.

"Stop looking at each other like that, for goodness' sake," she said.

Max and I freaked out.

"Mum?" I asked, looking desperately around the tiny shack. "Where are you?"

"Hmm," said Mum, giving it some thought. "This is going to sound odd but I think I might be in your heads."

"Whose head?" said Max, bewildered.

"Both your heads," she said. "I seem to be able to switch between them. Right now I'm looking out of your eyes, Max, at Flo, who looks rather confused. And now I'm looking out of Flo's eyes and yes, you look just as confused, Max."

And then the penny finally dropped. "Of course!" I shouted. "How could I forget? *Last to Leave* has a spectator mode."

Video Game Tip: In spectator mode eliminated players are able to watch the action unfolding from the point of view of their still-living teammates. Some might say the downside is that when you're trying to concentrate on winning the game, having your friends watching your every move and telling you what to do isn't always as helpful as they imagine it to be.

"This is great," said Max. "It means we're all still in the game together. If we win, your mum wins too and we leave together. Right?"

"I guess," I said. I sure hoped so. "We still have to win though."

Max checked his watch. "Another two players have been eliminated," he said. "There are only eleven left in the game."

He pulled up the map hologram. "Most of it's gone," he said, pointing to the swathes of black that had once contained the other zones.

"It's more dangerous now," I said. "But it's also easier to predict where the Void goes next. It looks like it's going to finish on the bridge. So we need to press on and get ourselves a decent spot because it's all going to kick off soon. How's your inventory looking?"

"I have a laser pistol with zero charge," said Max, "a tin-pan helmet riddled with holes and one health pack."

"You better heal up," I said. In the corner of the room was a charge pack. I handed it to Max. "Here, take this."

I wasn't exactly overflowing with laser charge

either, but I figured I probably had enough to last me until the end of the game. If we made it to the end. My helmet and armour were damaged but it could be worse. I also had a single health pack.

"You ready?" I asked him.

Max took a long breath, then nodded.

"Good luck, you two!" said Mum.

"Let's do this," I said, kicking open the door.

A woman in a firefighter's outfit was running

straight towards us. Two blasts from my laser cannon and she was gone.

We ran towards the bridge, ducking and dodging laser fire the whole way. I saw a couple of crates at the start of the bridge that looked like a good place to take cover. When we got there, a man jumped out from behind them. He may have been dressed as a cowboy but he wasn't a faster draw than me.

"Nice shooting," said Max, as we crouched behind the boxes. "The firefighter and the cowboy bring the number of players down to nine. So that's seven other players still left."

Max and I flinched at the sound of laser blasts, before realizing they were coming from the other side of the river, across the bridge. I peered over the top of the crate. In the distance I could just make out a single player, running towards the bridge, shooting, rolling, jumping, spinning, twirling and twisting in every direction. One by one the players shooting at him were falling. I looked through the binoculars and saw a black fringe covering most of his face.

"It's Hodges," I said.

"Are you sure?" asked Mum.

"Positive," I said.

"He's just taken out a squad of four by himself," said Max. "What if this comes down to us versus him?"

"Then we'll need to be at our best," I said. I checked my charge and realized I was almost empty. "Better reload now."

I was midway through changing over the charge pack when I saw something moving to my right. I spun round to see a girl dressed as an astronaut come out from underneath the bridge, two laser pistols pointing right at me. With my laser cannon still reloading I was a sitting duck. It was over.

"Flo, look out!" shouted Mum.

PEW-PEW!

The girl vanished. I turned round to see Max, open-mouthed, pointing his laser pistol at where the girl had just been.

"Max, you did it!" I said.

Max grinned. "I did, didn't I?"

"All this time I was worrying about you and you were actually a crack shot!" I said.

"Flo, over there!" Mum yelled, and an instant later I realized a man dressed as a superhero had appeared behind us. Two shots struck Max in the back, knocking him to the ground. I returned fire instantly but the super nuisance started bunny-hopping about the place, dodging all my shots.

"Flo, are you going to heal me?" asked Max as I kept firing. "It's just I can see a counter on my watch and I don't think I have much time left."

"I can't heal you until I take care of him," I said. "Because then he'll take me out and eliminate us both."

"Right," said Max. "Fair point."

"Hey, nice shooting!" The other player laughed as he bounced around the place. "NOT!"

"Ugh, stay still," I said, trying to line him up.

Two blasts came from the other side of the bridge, striking Super Nuisance in the chest. He vanished.

I looked across the bridge. It was Hodges, his avatar doing a wave emote at me. He must have found a scope attachment, to fire from that distance.

I turned back to Max – but he'd disappeared.

"Too late," he said.

"Never mind, Max," said Mum reassuringly. "You did very well."

"Thanks, Ms Waters," said Max.

"Great, now I have both of you in my head." I sighed.

I looked at my watch.

Two players were left.

I looked across the bridge. On the other side, waiting, was Hodges.

LEVEL 11

"I can't watch this. It's too tense," said Max as I stepped on to the bridge. "How do you close your eyes in here?"

"I don't think you can," said Mum. "Sweetheart, be careful. Not to put any pressure on you but literally everything depends on you winning right now."

"Thanks, Mum, that's really helping," I said sarcastically.

"What's your game plan?" asked Max, sounding panicked. Before I could respond he added, "You should find cover. He's got that long-range weapon so he could hit you from all the way over there. Why are you just walking towards him, Flo? Why are you putting away your laser cannon, Flo? Flo?"

"Max, relax. I know what I'm doing," I said. This wasn't completely true but I did have an idea and it was worth trying. It would be either the cleverest or the dumbest thing I'd ever done. "If he was going to shoot me, he would have already done it."

As I walked towards Hodges I could see him doing the same, but unlike me he kept his laser cannon up and locked firmly in my direction. Around us the Void kept creeping closer. The bridge itself was now the only firm part of the map left. One way or another this would be over soon.

"Are you trying to throw the game or something?" shouted Hodges as we met in the middle.

I shook my head. "No," I said. "I was hoping I could convince you to do that."

Hodges laughed. "Me throw the game? And help you win? You had your chance for me to help you, Waters, and you blew it. Now, let's get this over with. Take out your laser cannon, will you? At least make it a fair fight. I don't want to blast you when you're unarmed."

Instead of arming my laser cannon, I tossed it down at his feet.

"That only works if the other person doesn't already have a gun," said Hodges. "And even if I didn't, there's obviously no charge in it. It's a trick."

"It's not a trick," I said. "There's half a charge still in there. Enough that I could have taken you down if I'd wanted to."

Hodges snorted. "As if."

"But I didn't because I don't know what's going to happen if we win this game," I said. "We need someone in the real world to know the truth. Someone we can trust."

Hodges' avatar remained motionless and silent for several seconds. "What are you talking about?" he asked.

"You really want to know why winning this game is so important to me?" I said. "Here goes. The truth."

I told him everything. The Digital Imprint Scanner in Mum's workshop. How we defeated him in *Star Smasher*. Taking down Carl with Girdy and the other monsters in *Blocktopia*. Winning the *Critter Clash* tournament with Hungrabun and Kiwi. And finally, Mum entering *Last to Leave* to try and get us home.

Of course I had to talk pretty fast to fit everything

in, given the threat of the Void closing in on us in a matter of minutes. After I was done I waited for Hodges to speak.

"How gullible do you think I am?" he asked.

"It's true," I said. "We really are stuck in this video game."

"Right, right," he said. "You and your mum and Mark."

"My name isn't Mark, it's Max!" screamed Max.

"Stop yelling, Max," I said. "He can't hear you."

Hodges' avatar made a yawning emote. "You're going to have to try harder than that," he said.

"But I can prove it," I said. "Haven't you noticed that I can do things this video game doesn't let you do? Like when I hugged my mum."

"That was just an emote that I've never seen before," said Hodges.

"OK, give me something you know for sure you can't do in this video game then," I said.

Hodges considered for a few seconds, then said, "You can't fart."

"Fart?" I repeated.

"Yep," said Hodges. "They won't allow it in the game because some parents got mad about it. I even started an online petition to get it added and got enough signatures that the Prime Minister had to talk about it in Parliament."

"All right, give me a second then," I said.

"Flo … you're not honestly about to—" said Mum.

PAAAAAARRRRRRRPPPPPP!!!

Hodges' avatar just stared at me.

"So glad games don't have smells," said Max.

"You … really are in the game," said Hodges.

"I really am," I said. "And so is Max and my mum

and we need your help. Mum's built some kind of program that she thinks could get us out as long as we win."

Hodges used a nodding emote. "You need me to let you win?"

"Yeah," I said. "But I need something else. There's a chance this might not work. If it doesn't then you're the only person in the real world who knows we're trapped. You'll have to try and get help. You'll be our only hope at that point. And … Max's mum and dad… You'll need to let them know. Tell them I'm sorry."

I looked away. I wasn't even entirely sure if crying was possible in the game, but for the second time in a matter of minutes I did feel the need to rub my eyes. I could see the Void creeping on to the bridge itself. The land it had been attached to was no longer there so the bridge was just floating in mid-air. Sometimes video games really didn't make a whole lot of sense. I think that's why I loved them so much.

"Flo, there's not much time," said Hodges. "Quickly, why does your mum think you winning the game will work this time when it hasn't worked before?"

"Um … Mum?" I asked.

"Tell him that the new software I've written intercepts on a GRS – that's a Game Reset Sequence," said Mum. "It's the only point at which the security of the game's code is temporarily reduced, since most of the code is in the process of being deleted anyway. We have to win the game to trigger the GRS."

I relayed this to Hodges as best as I could.

"No, she's wrong!" he said.

"I'm what?" said Mum.

"She's what?" I said.

"Wrong," he repeated. "Not about the GRS or the drop in security – that's all true. But the bit about winning the game to trigger it, that's wrong."

"What do you mean?" I asked as the Void continued to move in. The bridge was already half gone.

"The game doesn't reset when you win," said Hodges. "Think about it. Every game tracks your progress. You win, it updates your win/loss record, how many people you took out – all your stats. The game doesn't reset, it just moves on. If it didn't then you might as well intentionally lose the game because that would do the same thing."

My mouth was hanging open.

"Is that true?" asked Max.

"I'm not sure," said Mum. "It … it might be."

"Are you saying there's nothing we can do?" I asked Hodges. "It doesn't matter if we win or lose?"

"There might be another way," he said. "But you'd have to trust me."

"What?" I said.

"We crash the game," said Hodges.

I held my head in my hands. We were doomed.

"Hear me out," said Hodges. "I know a way to do it. And when games crash, G-Locker's recovery mode kicks in, which will trigger *Last to Leave*'s GRS. It'll reset the game!"

I looked at Hodges doubtfully. "You know how to crash the game? Another hack, I'm guessing?"

"Not a hack," said Hodges. "More of a bug that I've known about for some time. I never saw much of a use for it before."

Only a quarter of the bridge was left now.

"Hurry," I said.

"In *Last to Leave* there are always winners and losers," he said, talking much faster now. "If the players don't decide that among themselves then the Void will. In that case the winner is whoever had the most health when the Void hits. It's like a tie-breaker. But what if it comes down to two people on opposite teams and the Void hits them at the exact same time and they both have the exact same amount of health? The game designers never figured that could happen so they didn't program for it."

"So you're saying we don't try to win or lose?" I said. "We play for a draw?"

"Exactly," said Hodges.

Time was almost up and darkness was all around us. A decision had to be made but I knew I couldn't do it without asking the others.

"Mum, Max, what do you think?" I asked.

"Crashing the game?" said Max. "We might never come back from that. At least if we win, we might jump back to *Star Smasher* or *Blocktopia* or *Critter Clash*."

"Max is right," said Mum. "What Hodges is saying makes sense but I can't verify any of it. I suppose it comes down to how much you trust he knows what he's talking about."

That was it, wasn't it? How much did I trust Hodges?

"I trust him," I said.

I took out my last health pack. "What's your health like?" I asked Hodges.

"Full," he said. "You use it."

I nodded then felt a tingle as I returned to full strength. The Void was a couple of metres away now and it seemed to me that the only light left in the entire universe was hovering above the small circle of land that we stood upon.

"OK," I said. "Let's do it."

I stuck my hand out to Hodges and he did a shake emote. A second later the Void hit and the last of the light was finally snuffed out. Everything went black.

Then red.

Then green.

Then blue.

And then… There, in giant neon multi-coloured letters, tumbling all around us, were the words:

END LEVEL

Three months later…

Max and I were sitting on the couch in my living room, watching a film on the TV. Max was staying for Sunday dinner and there was a delicious smell of the roast wafting around the house. The film was about a secret agent who had to stop some bad guy from crashing the Moon into the Earth.

And I was bored out of my mind.

"Hey, Max," I said. "Do you fancy a quick game? We could even play *Blocktopia* if you want."

The fact that I was suggesting my least favourite

game was a reflection of how bad the film was.

"For the hundredth time, no!" said Max. "I told you the moment we got out of *Last to Leave* that I'm never playing another game as long as I live. I'm done with them."

I let out a massive sigh. Max had kept his word about learning to say 'no' to me. I couldn't get him to do anything these days.

"I'd much rather sit and watch a nice movie where I don't have to do anything and there's no chance of me getting sucked in," added Max. He suddenly sat up. "Wait… Your mum hasn't made any modifications to your TV, has she?"

I rolled my eyes. "No," I said.

Max relaxed and slumped back into the couch. "Where is she anyway?" he asked.

"With Hodges, working on their secret project."

After we had escaped the game, Mum offered to teach Hodges about programming and engineering since he clearly had a knack for it with his hacking background. Now he came round most weekends and sometimes after school for lessons. Occasionally Hodges and I would play games together, which was actually pretty cool since he's ALMOST as good as me. Obviously I'd never tell him that. He already has a pretty high opinion of himself. He should really learn to be more modest, like me.

We haven't really played games as much recently though. He and Mum have apparently hit a breakthrough in their project. They promised to tell me more about it soon, but I'm still waiting.

If I'm honest, I wasn't that bothered about no one playing games with me. I hardly played them myself any more, even single-player ones. When you had actually lived the games it just wasn't the same playing them with a controller, watching them unfold on a screen. Plus I couldn't play any that involved me fighting non-player characters now. Having actually become friends with a few of them it was impossible to think of them as just pixels any more.

I left Max to the film and wandered along to Mum's workshop. The door was slightly ajar and I could see that the lights were off. I poked my head in but there was no sign of Mum or Hodges. This wasn't unusual – Mum had a lot of equipment that overflowed into the garage or the garden shed, so they'd most likely be in one of those two places.

Still, given what had happened recently in this workshop I knew I should probably double check.

I stepped into the darkened room and headed towards the bench where Mum had kept the Digital

Imprint Scanner. It was still there – the goggles of the device staring silently back at me. The first thing Mum had done when we had jumped out of *Last to Leave* was cut every wire in the scanner.

Every now and then though, I did think about what it would be like to use the device again. To go back and visit some of the friends we'd made in the games or even make new ones. When I thought about all the worlds out there waiting for us…

"Flo!"

"AAAARRRRGHHHHH!" I screamed, almost jumping out of my skin. I spun round and saw Hodges standing there, a mad grin on his face.

"Don't sneak up on people like that!" I told him.

"Sorry," he laughed. "I was looking for you."

"You were?" I said, my heart returning to its normal speed. "What for?"

"We've finished!" he said. "The project. It's ready. You have to come see this."

"All right," I said. I took one last look at the DIS and noticed something. Its side was hanging partway off. I pulled open the case, only to find a few cut wires and nothing else. All the circuit boards had been removed.

"What happened—" I began.

"Come on, you'll see," Hodges interrupted.

Hodges escorted me not to the garage or the shed as I had expected, but to the kitchen. Mum was waiting for us, sitting at the table in front of her laptop, which was connected to several strange-looking circuit boards. Wires were snaking all over the table.

"Ah, you're here," she said.

"What's going on?" I asked.

"Well," she said. "As you know, after the Digital Imprint Scanner fiasco, I was certainly never going to let anyone else use the device. Clearly it's far too dangerous. But the fact that you were able to jump between games and interact with all the characters in those games got us thinking about other uses for the technology."

"The DIS allows people in our world to join any game," continued Hodges. "So what if we could do the same thing for the characters in the games themselves?"

I looked at them blankly. "You've lost me," I said.

"This might explain it better," said Mum. She pressed a button on the laptop and the familiar island of *Last to Leave* flickered into view. There was a game in progress, a colourful team of four driving across a field in an open-top sports car.

I let out a gasp.

I recognized that team. I knew that team.

In the driver's seat sat Gary, the reluctant Space Soldier from *Star Smasher*.

Next to him was Girdy, the giant Boulder Person from *Blocktopia*.

And in the back were a tiny rabbit-like critter called Hungrabun and an equally small bird named Kiwi – the two creatures Max and I had briefly coached while trapped in *Critter Clash*.

"What…? How…? What?" I stammered.

"We were able to repurpose the DIS to allow characters to cross over to any game you want," said Mum.

"That's… That's … AMAZING!" I said.

"We thought you'd like it," said Hodges. "But your mum didn't want to tell you before it was ready, in case—"

"I got impatient and pressed something I shouldn't?" I asked.

"More or less," said Mum.

"This is so cool," I said, watching the screen. Then I noticed that in the right-hand bottom corner there were two tiny lines of text:

STABLE MODE ‹

EXPERIMENTAL MODE

"Hey, what's experimental mode?" I said, pressing the down arrow. The little cursor switched.

Mum's and Hodges' faces turned white.

"I thought you removed that option?" said Mum.

"I thought you said you were going to do it," said Hodges.

"Calm down," I said. "Nothing's happened—"

The lights started flickering in the room and the

laptop screen went black. Then, after a few seconds the flickering stopped and the screen lit up again.

The three of us looked at each other.

"We all still seem to be here, so that's good," said Hodges.

"Maybe I'll just switch this back to stable mode," I said.

"I think that's a good idea," said Mum.

As my hand hovered over the up arrow, I looked at the screen again. There was something odd about it. The sports car had come to a stop in the middle of a road and the four characters were nowhere to be seen.

Suddenly there was a scream from the living room.

"Max!" I shouted as the three of us rushed through the house.

We burst into the living room to find Max pressed up against the wall, gaping in astonishment.

He wasn't alone.

"Flo!" shouted Gary, giving me a great big hug in his hulking space armour. "So good to see you again!"

"Nice place you got here," said Girdy, whose head had punctured a hole in the ceiling.

Hungrabun and Kiwi had climbed on to the couch and Hungrabun was flicking through the TV channels with the remote. "You got the sports channels on this thing?" she asked.

"What's that horrible smell?" asked Kiwi, sniffing the air. "Smells like someone's cooking a bird or something."

I looked at Mum.

"All right," she said. "No one panic. I think I know how to fix this…"

I grinned.

FIND OUT HOW

THE ADVENTURE

BEGAN IN...

LEVEL 1

"Are you sure we should be doing this?" whispered Max as we tiptoed into my mum's workshop. The place was littered with all kinds of junk – broken electronics, piles of circuit boards and brightly coloured wires snaking all over the place. We had to take great care not to trip over Mum's half-finished projects.

"Yeah, of course," I said, stepping over the remains of a toaster. "Why?"

"It's just that we're talking really quietly and tiptoeing about," he said. "Which doesn't usually mean that we're allowed to do something. Also, there's a cardboard sign over there that says *Don't even think about it, Flo*."

"There is not…" I said, before spotting the sign myself. It was propped up against a bulky metal device, with what looked like part of an eyepiece peeking out from behind it. I gave Max a reassuring laugh. "Oh, that's just Mum's sense of humour. You know what scientists are like. She's always leaving daft signs around. *Don't leave the fridge door open, Flo* or *Don't forget to wash your hands after going to the toilet, Flo*. Honestly, you shouldn't take her seriously."

Max frowned. "You don't wash your hands?"

"Of course I do," I said, rolling my eyes. "But she wants me to do it *every* time. I'm not the blinking Queen, am I?"

"Well ... no..." admitted Max. "But..."

"Exactly. Besides, have I ever led you astray?"

"All the time," he said, nodding vigorously. "Pretty much every day of my life."

"*Every* day?" I repeated doubtfully.

"Fine, not *every* day," he conceded. "You did go on holiday for a week last year, so..."

"Ugh, you're such an exaggerator. Let's just take a look at this machine and then we can go," I said, grabbing the sign and flinging it away. But behind it was another piece of card that read, *I'm serious, Flo. Under no circumstances should you touch this device until I tell you it's ready.*

"What a joker," I said, flinging that one away too. There were another couple of signs after that, but I didn't even bother reading those. "What have we got then?"

It was a metal box about the size of my head.
Sticking out of the top was a pair of black goggles,
with what looked like a chin rest underneath them.
A cable at the back of the box was connected to
my mum's computer, which was currently powered
down.

"Looks like one of those machines opticians use," I said. "The ones that blow air into your eyes to test if you can keep them open when it's windy."

"That's to test for glaucoma," Max pointed out, pushing his specs up his nose.

"This machine *definitely* doesn't do that," I said. "Hardly anyone I know has got one. Only that puffed-up poser Rhett Hodges."

Max nodded. "Great," he said, without much enthusiasm. "Sounds good."

"You have no idea what it is, do you?" I said.

"None whatsoever," he admitted.

I let out a groan. "You know Hodges, right? The older kid from school?"

"Yeah," sighed Max. "You never stop going on about him. He's like the biggest game streamer in the country or something. And he always beats you at video games."

I could feel my face go bright red. "He does not always beat me!" I snapped.

"Shhh!" said Max. "Your mum might hear us."

"Fine, but he doesn't *always* beat me at video games," I said. "Besides, he only ever plays *Star Smasher*. Well, used to play it anyway. He stopped streaming after I finally beat him. Though conveniently his stream cut out right before anyone could see it happen."

"Yeah, that was convenient..." said Max, letting the thought trail off.

"Are you saying I'm making it up?" I put my hands on my hips.

Max fell silent.

"People thought he was great because he was able to buy amazing equipment with all the money he got from streaming," I said. "If Mum would just let me start my own stream then maybe I'd be able to buy a DIS too."

Max scratched his chin. "A DIS?"

"A Digital Imprint Scanner," I said. "They've just come out and they're amazing. Basically they scan your DNA and turn it into computer code."

Max continued to scratch his chin. "I see. What for, exactly?"

Max didn't really get computers and games the way I did. Sometimes things that seemed perfectly obvious to me, he just didn't have a clue about. It was like talking to most grown-ups.

"Imagine being able to see yourself in any video game ever made," I said. "That's what the device does. Some games come with editors that let you change how your avatar looks, so maybe after a few hours of changing gazillions of body parts, you finally end up with someone who kind of looks like you if you squint really hard. But this thing does all the work for you. For *any* game. Even ones that wouldn't normally let you change your character. It's amazing. But it's also super expensive."

Max looked at the device sitting on the table. "Your mum bought you one?"

I shook my head. "Mum's a scientist for the government, remember," I said. "She can't afford to buy me one. But when I told her about it, she got pretty excited. She figured she could build one herself. The problem is she won't let me use it until it's ready."

"That's probably sensible, isn't it?" asked Max.

Not only did he not get video games, Max didn't get my mum. "No," I said firmly. "You don't understand. I mean, don't get me wrong, Mum is a genius. But the problem is she never finishes anything. Look around you. She starts building all these cool things but she never completes them. She just keeps tinkering with them until she has a new idea, then switches to that. I'll be waiting forever for her to finish this."

Max didn't look convinced. "I don't know, Flo, I think you should probably hold off..."

Ignoring him, I switched on Mum's computer, which was lightning-fast. She'd fitted it with loads of upgrades – tons of memory, a cutting-edge graphics card and a solid-state hard drive. It was great for playing games on.

It only took a few seconds to fire up. When it did, instead of the usual login screen, I was presented with a text prompt:

>BOOT UP FLO-SCAN OS V0.01? Y/N

"Flo-scan?" I said, smiling. "She named it after me. Cool!" I pressed the *Y* key and watched as a bunch of ones and zeros scrolled up the screen. After a few moments, a green light flickered on the front of the device that was connected to the computer, accompanied by a strange whirring noise. On screen, the numbers disappeared, replaced by another prompt:

>WHEN READY, PLEASE PLACE CHIN ON THE REST AND LOOK DIRECTLY INTO THE LENS

"Right, here goes," I said. Pressing my chin against the plastic, I looked right into the eyepiece and...

Nothing.

"Why's it not doing anything?" I asked.

"That's odd. It's like it's not finished," said Max sarcastically.

I raised my head and looked at the screen again.

"It looks pretty cool, though," said Max, clearly trying to make me feel better. He placed his own chin on the rest. "I'm sure it'll be great when it's ready."

"Maybe you need to do something else," I muttered to myself, looking down at the keyboard. I pushed the *Enter* key.

COLLECT THEM ALL
AND GET READY TO

TOM NICOLL

The only way out is to win...

LEVEL UP!

ILLUSTRATED BY
ANJAN SARKAR

TOM NICOLL

LEVEL UP!

BLOCK AND ROLL

ILLUSTRATED BY
ANJAN SARKAR

TOM NICOLL

LEVEL UP!

BEAST BATTLES

ILLUSTRATED BY
ANJAN SARKAR

TOM NICOLL

LEVEL UP!

LAST ONE STANDING

ILLUSTRATED BY
ANJAN SARKAR

ACKNOWLEDGEMENTS

There are a lot of people to thank for this series. If I forget anyone it's only because I have a terrible memory, not because I'm not grateful. We cool? OK.

Huge thanks to my brilliant editor Mattie, who through the simple act of always being right, made these books so much better.

Thanks to Anjan for bringing Flo and Max to life with his amazing illustrations.

And thanks to Katie for going to bat for the series in the first place, as well as all her help over the years to make me a better writer.

Thanks to all the ridiculously talented people at Little Tiger, past and present, who worked on the series including my copyeditor Anna, proofreaders Susila and Ella and designers Paul,

Jack, Harriet, Shona and Pip. And to Charlie, Lauren and Leilah for all their work and support in promoting me and my silly books.

Thanks to my awesome agent Jodie, whose surname I accidentally borrowed for Flo's nemesis because it was the only one I could get a decent anagram out of. And to Emily and Molly too.

Thanks to my parents, mostly for buying me that ZX Spectrum for Christmas in 1990, which led to my love of computer games. There's probably other stuff they did but that's the main one I can think of.

Thanks to my wife and best friend Kaye for all her love and support for the last fifteen years. Thanks to Eilidh and Molly for being the best and sleeping through the night.

And thanks to the Squad aka the Carnivores aka Barry White and the Chipmunks – David, Andy and Sandy – for all the Friday Night Games, Chicken Dinners and the Battle Royale "research". Andy, you left me on that bike to die but I forgive you, man. I forgive you.

Finally, thanks to all the kids who have read my books and the schools that have invited me to come talk to their pupils. It was visiting schools and seeing how excited kids would get whenever video games were mentioned that led to me writing this series in the first place. So I suppose what I'm saying is: if you haven't enjoyed the series, blame them not me.

– Tom

ABOUT THE AUTHOR

Tom Nicoll has been writing since he was in school, where he enjoyed trying to fit as much silliness in his essays as he could possibly get away with. When not writing, he enjoys playing video games (especially the ones where he gets beaten by kids half his age from all over the world). He is also a big comedy, TV and movie nerd. Tom lives just outside Edinburgh with his wife and two daughters.

LEVEL UP: LAST ONE STANDING
is his twelfth book for children.

ABOUT THE ILLUSTRATOR

Anjan Sarkar first realized he loved illustration as a child when, with a few strokes of a crayon, he drew a silly face that made his mum laugh. Silly faces are funny and make people laugh, he thought. Since then, he's grown up into a hairy-faced man who draws silly faces for a living (not just for his mum). When he's not drawing he likes walking in the countryside and eating biscuits (sometimes he does both at the same time). Anjan lives in Sheffield with his wife and two kids.